MW01154602

Unicorn Coloring Book For Adults

Unicorn Coloring Book featuring various Unicorn designs filled with stress relieving patterns.

Coloring Books For Adults: Vol 9

by The Coloring Book People

ISBN-13: 978-1535176163

ISBN-10: 1535176164

PREVIEW

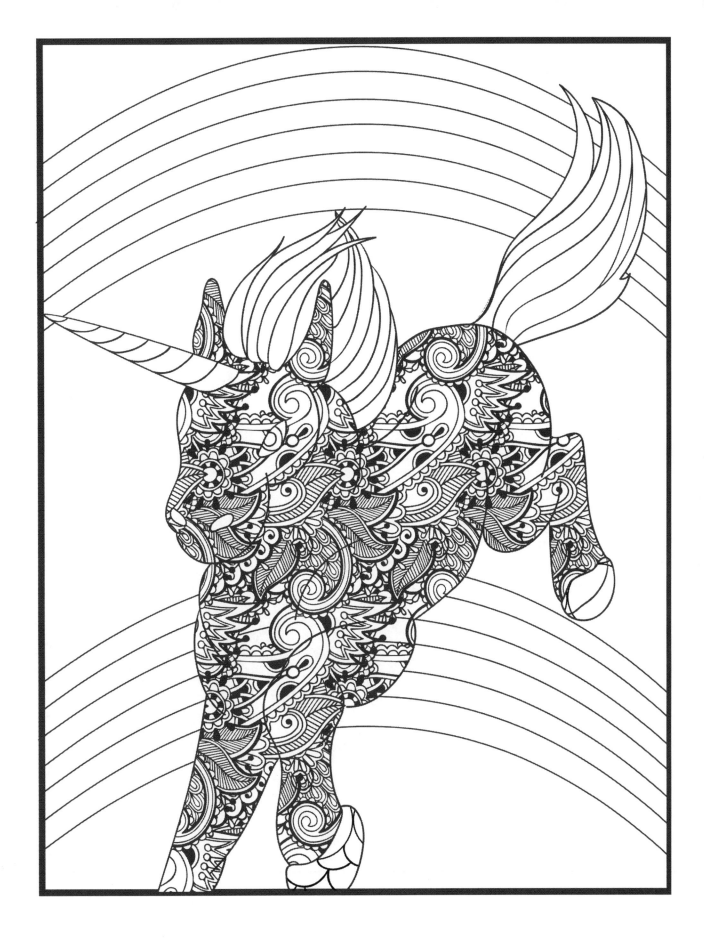

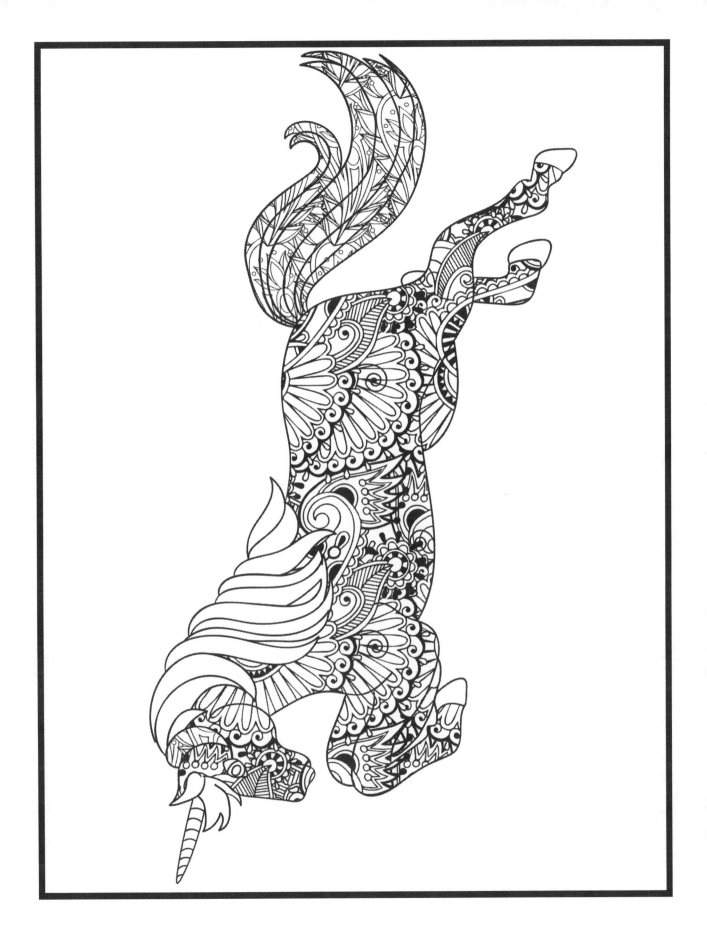

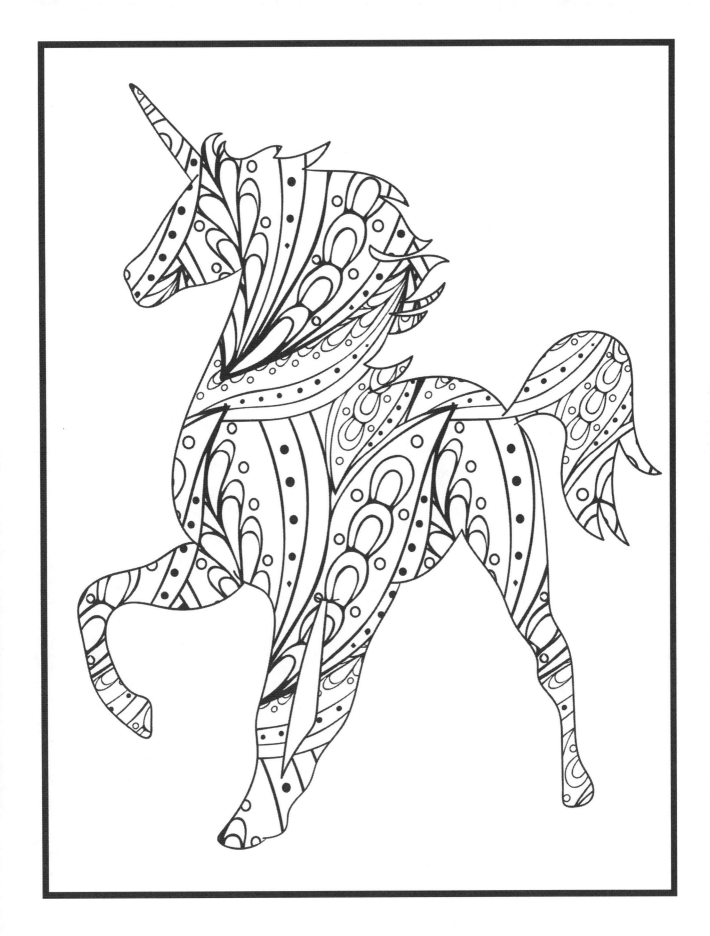

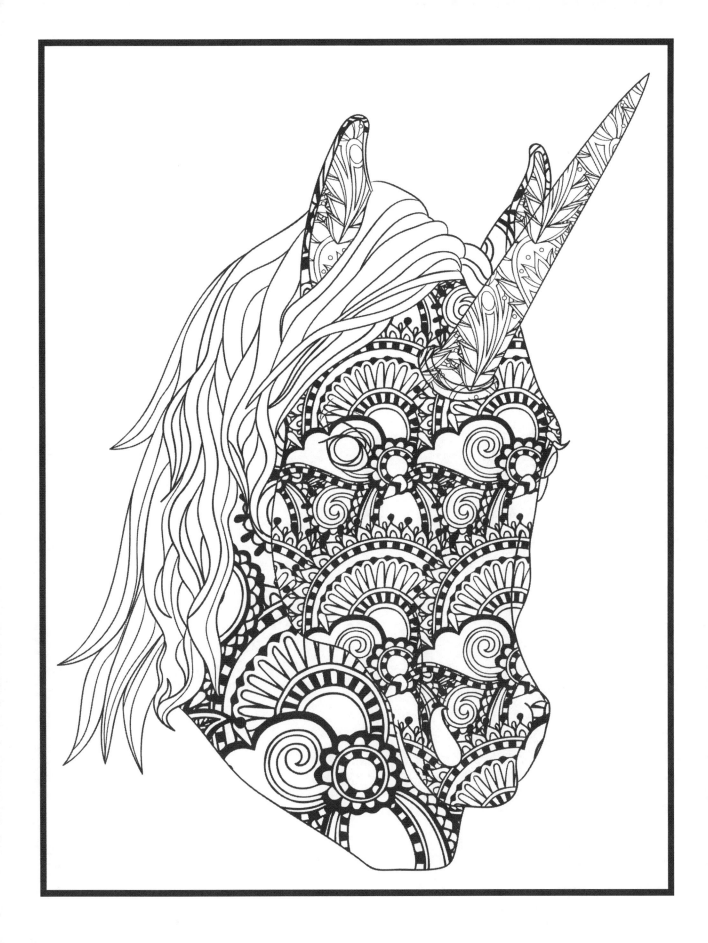

COLOR TEST PAGE

COLOR TEST PAGE

Made in the USA
San Bernardino, CA
14 August 2016